Nate the Great and The Tardy TorToise

Nate the Great
and The
Tardy
TorToise

by Marjorie Weinman Sharmat
and Craig Sharmat

illusTraTed by Marc SimonT

A YEARLING BOOK

Published by
Yearling
an imprint of
Random House Children's Books
a division of Random House, Inc.
New York

Visit us on the Web! www.randomhouse.com/kids

Educators and librarians, for a variety of teaching tools, visit us at www.randomhouse.com/teachers

ISBN-13: 978-0-440-41269-4
ISBN-10: 0-440-41269-2

Reprinted by arrangement with Delacorte Press
Printed in the United States of America
One Previous Edition
New Yearling Edition July 2005
40   39   38
UPR

For my parents,
who patiently took me
under their shell

—C.S.

I, Nate the Great, am a detective.
This morning I did not have
a case to solve.
I woke up late.
I stretched.
My dog, Sludge, stretched.

We looked out the window.
The sun was shining.
The birds were singing.
A tortoise was eating.
A tortoise was eating
the flowers in my garden.

I do not own a tortoise.
Sludge does not
own a tortoise.
Sludge and I rushed out
to the backyard.
The tortoise started to eat
a petunia.
A bite here.
A bite there.
He started to eat a daisy.
A bite here.
A bite there.
I, Nate the Great,
like to look at flowers.
Soon there would not be
any flowers to look at.

I stared at the tortoise.

He was green.

He had a thick shell.

And a big appetite.

He did not have any teeth.

But he did good work without them.

I knew I must take him away.

But what would I
do with him?

"You must live somewhere," I said.

"You must have an address
and a telephone number."

I knew that a tortoise can live
for a very long time.

This tortoise could be
a hundred years old.

He should know where he lives by now.

He started to crawl away.

Slowly.

Very, very slowly.

Was he on his way home?

No. He was on his way
to eat my violets.

This tortoise was lost.

He needed help.

I said, "I, Nate the Great,
have never taken a case
for anyone who is green
and has a thick shell.
But I must find out
where you live
and take you there."
I got dressed.
I wrote a note to my mother.

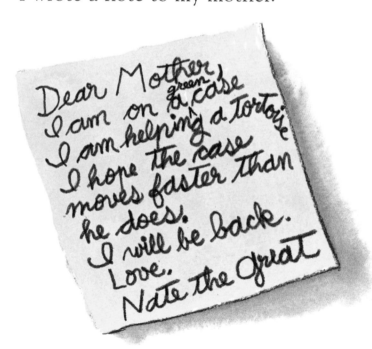

I, Nate the Great, got a box.
I put lots of holes in it.
Then I put the tortoise in the box.
"I am taking you home,"
I said. "Wherever that is."
Where *was* his home?
I was thinking.
This tortoise is slow.
Perhaps he did not crawl
very far from home.

Perhaps he lives near here.
But he knows how to find food.
He could have been crawling
and eating for days.
He could have eaten his way
from the other side of town.
This tortoise could live anywhere!
I spoke to Sludge.
"This is a strange pet.
Who would own a strange pet?"
Sludge knew the answer.

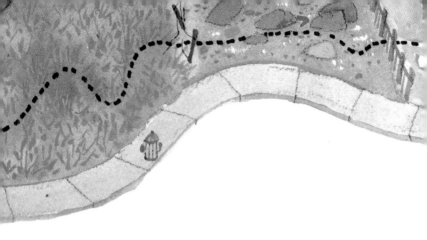

We rushed to Rosamond's house
with the box.
We walked
up the front steps.
Sludge sniffed
the steps.
Step by step.
I bent down to see
what Sludge was sniffing.
It was a trail of crumbs.
They led to the front door.
Sludge scratched on the door.

Rosamond opened it.
She was holding two crumbling
cupcakes.
Her cats, Little Hex, Plain Hex,

Big Hex, and Super Hex, were
eating crumbs from the floor.
"I have brought over
a lost pet," I said.
"Why, thank you," Rosamond said.
She opened the box
and saw the tortoise.
"This is not a cat,"
she said. "It is green
and has a shell.
I do not want it."
"This is not a gift," I said.
"I found this tortoise and
I am looking for his home.
Do you know anybody who
has lost a pet?"
"I heard that Claude lost
something," Rosamond said.

"But I don't know what it is.
Claude is always losing things."
"You are losing your cupcakes,"
I said. "They are turning
into crumbs."
"These are tuna fish cupcakes,"

Rosamond said. "Want some?"
I, Nate the Great, had not
eaten breakfast.
I was hungry.
But I was not *that* hungry.
Sludge was licking up the crumbs.
It was time to leave.
I said good-bye to Rosamond.
Sludge sniffed his way
down the steps.

Then we went to Claude's house.

Claude opened the door.

I stared at him.

There was something missing.

He was not wearing a sock
on his left foot.

"Have you lost a tortoise?" I asked.

"No," Claude said. "I have lost
my sock."

"Do you know anybody who owns
a tortoise?"

"I know that Pip and Oliver
and Esmeralda and Annie
do not own a tortoise,"
Claude said. "They do not
have my sock either.
Can you look for it?"

"I, Nate the Great,
am on a case.
I must find out
where a tortoise lives."
"My case is bigger," Claude said.
"My sock is size eleven
and a half."

"I cannot look for it,"
I said.
"I will give you a clue,"
Claude said. "The sock matches
the one on my right foot."
"Good idea," I said.
Sludge and I walked away.
Claude yelled after us.

"If you find my sock,
and it doesn't look
as good as my right sock,
I don't want it.
I need a match."
I, Nate the Great,
needed some pancakes.
Sludge needed a bone.
We went home.

I took the tortoise out
of the box.
He crawled around the kitchen.
Slowly.
Very, very slowly.
I made pancakes.
I gave Sludge a bone.
The tortoise looked at me.
Was that a hungry look?
"You are full of flowers,"
I said.
He kept looking.
I gave him a piece of pancake.
He took a little bite.
"Your owner must wonder
where you are and when
you are coming home,"
I said. "You are one tardy tortoise."

I, Nate the Great,
ate a pancake and thought.
I needed a clue.
What did I know
about this tortoise?

Did he have any
friends or relatives?
How about hobbies?
I knew that he
liked flowers,
crawled very slowly,

and kept his secrets.

That was it.

This tortoise was never
going to get anywhere.

He was never going to be
President of the United States
or captain of the track team.

He was just a pet.

Like Sludge.

Hmmm.

Suddenly I knew what to do!
And where to look.

"This case is almost solved,"
I said to Sludge.

"I know who would know
where this tortoise lives."

I picked up the tortoise
and put him back in the box.

"Let's go," I said.
I, Nate the Great, and Sludge
rushed to the veterinarian
with the box.
"Tortoises must come here
just like most pets do," I said.
"There should be a record
of where this tortoise lives."
We walked into the waiting room.
It was full of dogs, cats,
and people.

The cats were meowing.

The dogs were barking.

One dog was barking the loudest.

It was Annie's dog, Fang.

He looked mad.

"Fang has a sore tooth,"

Annie said. "Look!"

I, Nate the Great,

did not want to look

at Fang's tooth.

"I am here on a case," I said.

I opened the box.
"I need to ask the vet
where this tortoise lives."
"Oh, a tortoise,"
Annie said. "I have
never seen one here."
"I have never seen one
here either," I said.

"But they do not meow.
They do not bark.
And they probably come
here in a box.
A tortoise could be here
and we would not see
or hear him."
"Yes," Annie said.
"But a tortoise is a reptile.
This place is not for reptiles,
birds, goldfish, goats, pigs,
wolves . . ."
"How do you know?" I asked.
"Because they thought Fang
was a wolf
the first time I brought him.
That's when I found out
who doesn't get in."

I, Nate the Great, sat down
next to a noisy cat.
This case was going
slower than the tortoise.
This case had come to
a dead end.
There was only one more thing
I could do.
I could get the name of
a reptile vet and go there.

And walk into a waiting room
filled with rattlesnakes,
boa constrictors, lizards,
alligators, crocodiles,
and other creepy creatures.
Some of them have
sharper fangs than Fang.
I had seen enough bites today.
I did not want to see any more.
Especially on me.

This case had begun with bites.

The tortoise was biting my flowers.

Biting . . .

Hmmm.

Perhaps that was a *clue*!

But what could I do with it?

I looked at Sludge.

He was the only dog in the room
who was not barking.

He was sniffing.
I thought about him sniffing
the trail of tuna fish
cupcake crumbs.
A *trail*.
Did *that* mean something?
All at once
I, Nate the Great, knew
that the tortoise
and Sludge
had given me the clues
I needed to solve this case.
We rushed home.
We went into the backyard.
I pulled out my magnifying glass.
"We are looking for a trail,"
I said. "A trail of bite marks.
On the flowers."

I looked to the right.
There were no bite marks.
I looked to the left.
I saw bite marks
shaped like little u's.
On flower after flower.

"Follow those u's!"
I said to Sludge.
"The tortoise ate his way
to our house. So we will
follow the trail
of bites backward
until we reach his house."
Sludge and I crept through
my garden.
Past the u's
on the petunias,
on the daisies.
On this flower and that flower.
Then the flowers stopped.
So did Sludge and I.
"The trail stops here,"
I said, "and the cement
walk starts. The tortoise

did not bite cement. We must
go to the yard next door."
Sludge and I rushed
to the next yard.
We saw flowers.
And we saw u's.
"This is easy," I said.
"This trail leads straight
to another yard."

Sludge and I made our way
to the next yard.
Then we stopped.
"This is *not* easy," I said.
"This yard has no flowers.
There are only weeds and grass.
Are they on the tortoise's menu?"
Sludge and I peered down.
We did not see any u's.
But we did see a trail.
Of dirt.
Where weeds had been.

Where grass had been.
The trail zigzagged.
Sludge and I zigzagged.
We zigzagged to
the other side of the yard.
The tortoise had munched
and crunched his way
from end to end.
Then the trail stopped.
More cement.
"On to the next yard," I said.
The next yard was full of rocks.
But I saw something bright
on the ground.
Was it part of a flower?
I bent down to look.
It was Claude's sock.
It was full of holes.

"I, Nate the Great,
have just solved a case
I did not want to solve.
And found a sock Claude
will never want to wear."
I picked up the sock
and put it in my pocket.

"Rocks and a sock," I said.

"This yard is no help.

The trail is cold.

But we will not give up.

On to the next yard!"

The next yard was full

of statues.

Snow White and the Seven Dwarfs.

Five flamingos.

And three ducks.

There was nothing alive

or green

or growing.

The tortoise could not

have eaten here.

"The trail is getting colder,"

I said. "Snow White,

the Seven Dwarfs, five flamingos,

and three ducks
cannot help us find
the tortoise's home.
But, I, Nate the Great,
will never give up."
Sludge wagged his tail.

We went to the next yard.
It was a mess.
I saw pieces of flowers.
Pieces of weeds.
Pieces of grass.
The yard had been
bitten to death!
Sludge and I looked
at each other.

"I, Nate the Great, say
that the tortoise
must have eaten
many meals in this yard.
This must be his
favorite restaurant."
And suddenly I knew why.
I saw a fence with a sign on it.
BEWARE OF THE TORTOISE.
I opened the box.
I spoke to the tortoise.
"Welcome home!" I said.
"The case is solved."
I took the tortoise
out of the box.

Suddenly a lady came
from behind the fence.
She ran toward us.
"Speedy, did you escape
under the fence again?
You are late for lunch."

Beware of
The Tortoise

"Lunch?" I thought.

"This tortoise never stopped
eating breakfast."

I handed Speedy to the lady.

Sludge's tail drooped.

He was sorry to see Speedy go.

So was I.

Speedy was a flower-wrecker,

a very slow mover,

and he had nothing to say.

But he was an okay tortoise.

"We will be back
to visit," I said.

"If you are here.

Remember where you live."

I reached into my pocket.

I pulled out Claude's sock.

I tied it to
the top of a stick.
I stuck the stick in the ground.
"A flag for you, Speedy.
This land is yours.
You ate it."
Then Sludge and I
and the empty box
started home.
Slowly.
Very, very slowly.

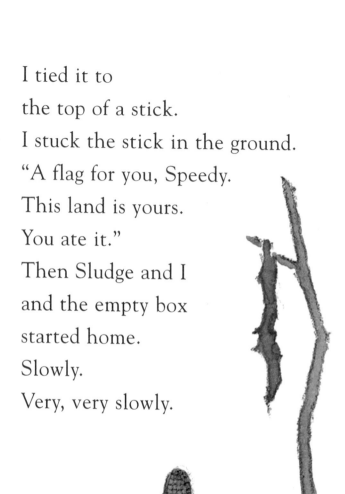

～Extra～
Fun Activities!

What's Inside

Nate knew tortoises were slow. He knew they ate a lot. Nate wanted to know more. He used the computer. He searched the Web. Here's some stuff he learned.

NATE'S NOTES:
Turtles, Tortoises—
What's the Difference?

Turtles and tortoises are closely related. There's not much difference between them.

BOTH TURTLES AND TORTOISES have hard shells. Both lay eggs. Both are cold-blooded. That means they can't control their body heat. Their bodies are cold in cold weather and warm in warm weather.

4

TURTLES live in (or near) the water. They know how to swim. Some have webbed feet like ducks. That helps them swim faster. Sea turtles live in the ocean. Other kinds of turtles live in ponds and lakes. During the winter, some turtles bury themselves in the mud. They sleep until the weather turns warm again.

TORTOISES live on land. They have short, stumpy feet. They eat shrubs, grasses, and even cactuses. Yow! When it gets hot, they dig holes and hide underground.

SHELL FACT: Some turtles and tortoises can pull their heads inside their shells. But they cannot climb out! Their shells are attached to their bodies.

NATE'S NOTES: Tortoise Talk

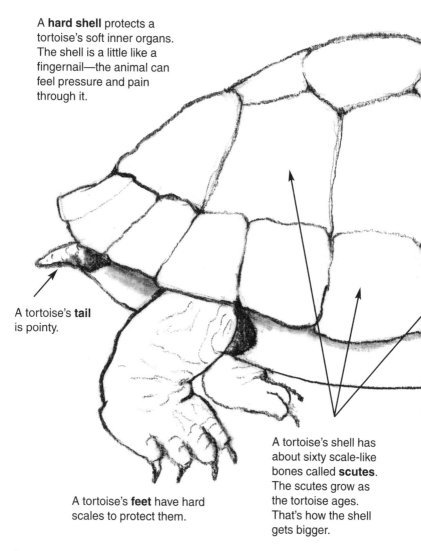

A **hard shell** protects a tortoise's soft inner organs. The shell is a little like a fingernail—the animal can feel pressure and pain through it.

A tortoise's **tail** is pointy.

A tortoise's **feet** have hard scales to protect them.

A tortoise's shell has about sixty scale-like bones called **scutes**. The scutes grow as the tortoise ages. That's how the shell gets bigger.

The **carapace** is the top of the shell.

The **seams** are the spots between the scutes.

A tortoise has a **nose** and a good sense of smell. This helps the tortoise find food. (But a tortoise has no real **ears**— just slits. Still, the animal can hear fine.)

The **plastron** is the shell's bottom. It is attached to the carapace with hinges.

NATE'S NOTES: Seven Interesting Turtles and Tortoises (Listed from Slow to Fast)

1. (Basically standing still): **Bog turtles** wander about—just barely. In a day, one was seen to travel just fifty-six feet. It took two weeks to cross a meadow.

2. (Very, very slow): **Wood turtles** take twenty-five minutes to walk 450 feet. At that speed, they'd need five hours to go a mile.

3. (Slow): Slightly faster are **giant tortoises**. In a speed test, the fastest plodded along at just .23 miles per hour. It would need about four hours to go one mile.

4. (Still slow, but moving): <u>**Gopherus tortoises**</u> have been clocked traveling fast enough to cover a mile in about three hours.

5. (Not so slow): **Cooters** are turtles that usually live in the water. Even on land, they can move at a respectable 1.07 miles per hour.

6. (Fast): Marine **green turtles** can swim 300 miles in ten days. That works out to about 1.25 miles an hour. Observers have clocked one moving 20 miles per hour. Whoa!

7. (Very, very fast): **A leatherback sea turtle** was once clocked swimming 22 miles per hour! That's about four times faster than the fastest human can swim! Forget hares! Watch out, sharks!

How to Make
a Sea Turtle Puppet

Puppets will not eat the flowers in your garden. This one will take a while to make. Take it slow. Take it steady. You will win in the end.

GET TOGETHER:

- two paper dessert plates
- a stapler
- a pencil
- a spoon to use as an outline
- green construction paper
- scissors
- a sponge
- white glue (like Elmer's)
- a straw
- a pair of craft eyes
- markers and crayons

MAKE YOUR SEA TURTLE PUPPET:

1. *Make the shell:* Put the plates together top to top, creating a rounded "shell." Staple the plates together with four evenly spaced staples.

2. *Make the feet:* With the pencil, trace the bowl of the spoon onto the paper. Repeat three more times. Cut out the four shapes. Glue the "feet" in place on the sides of the shell.

3. *Make the tail:* Cut a small triangle from the sponge. Glue it to one end of the straw.

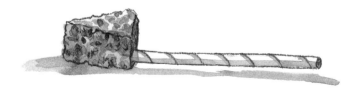

4. *Make the head:* Trace the spoon one more time. This time, create a "neck" by tracing about one inch up the spoon's handle. Carefully cut out the head and neck. Glue on the eyes.

5. Slip the straw between the plates. Pull it through so that the tail is just sticking out. You may need to trim the straw on the other end. You want about one inch of straw sticking out at both ends. Staple the head to the trimmed straw.

6. Decorate your shell with markers and crayons.

7. Pull the tail to make the turtle hide its head. Push the tail to make the head come out again.

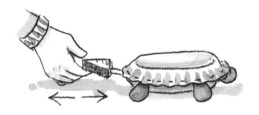

Turtle and Tortoise Jokes

Two snails crash. A turtle on the side of the road sees the whole thing. A police officer asks him what happened.

"I don't know!" the turtle says. "It all happened so fast!"

Why did the turtle cross the road?
It was the chicken's day off.

Why is turtle wax so expensive?
Because turtles have such tiny ears!

Why did the turtle cross the road?
To get to the shell station.

What did the snail riding on the tortoise's
back say?
Whee!

What was the tortoise doing on the highway?
About fifty inches per hour.

Where do you find a tortoise with no legs?
Wherever you left it!

What did the turtle wear to keep warm?
A turtleneck!

How to Make a Salad

(Perfect to Share with a Desert Tortoise)

*About forty breeds of tortoise slowly wander the earth.
They all love fruits and veggies. The desert tortoise lives
in the woods of the southwestern United States. It mostly
eats grass. But it also enjoys a salad once in a while.
Make this one. Share some with a tortoise (or a friend).*

Serves 2.

GET TOGETHER*:

- two bowls
- two big handfuls of cleaned spinach or
  watercress
- half a bell pepper (remove the seeds and cut
  into bite-sized pieces)
- a dozen or so baby carrots (slice into
  "pennies" or chunks)

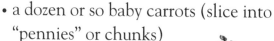

- a sprinkling of frozen peas or corn (let them warm up first)
- about a dozen cherry tomatoes (slice in half so they don't squirt when you bite them)
- half a pear (cut into bite-sized pieces)
- alfalfa or bean sprouts
- half a cucumber (slice into bite-sized pieces)

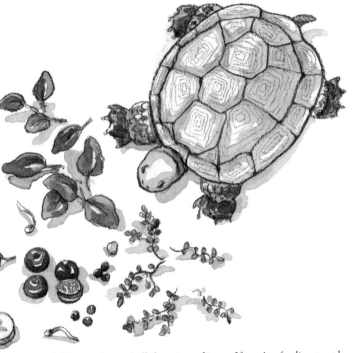

You don't need all these ingredients. If you're feeding people, use what you can get. But be careful with tortoises! Not all fruits and veggies are good for them.

MAKE YOUR SALAD:

1. Divide the spinach or watercress evenly between the bowls.
2. Put the rest of the fruits and veggies on top of the greens.
3. Serve with oil and vinegar or another salad dressing for humans. Tortoises prefer their salads dry!

How to Make Turtle Candies

Candy that looks like a turtle. Good stuff!

Ask an adult to help with this recipe. It will make twenty-four candies.

GET TOGETHER:

- a cookie sheet
- aluminum foil
- vegetable cooking spray
- 72 pecan halves (about 4 ounces)*
- 24 caramels, unwrapped
- 1 teaspoon butter
- 1 cup chocolate chips
- a pot with a heavy bottom
- a spoon

* If you don't like nuts, try popped popcorn.

MAKE YOUR TURTLE CANDIES:

1. Preheat the oven to 300 degrees.
2. Cover the cookie sheet with aluminum foil, shiny side up. Spray lightly with cooking spray.
3. Place 3 pecan halves in a clover shape on the foil. Put one caramel candy in the center of each clover.
4. Bake just until the caramel is melted. It should take 9 or 10 minutes.

5. Put the butter and the chocolate chips in the pot. Set over low heat until the chocolate chips are melted, and stir till blended.
6. Spoon the melted chocolate over the candies.
7. Pop in the fridge for half an hour.
8. Eat!

Talking Tortoise with a Keeper from the Knoxville Zoo

Michael Ogle is a zookeeper. He helps take care of the tortoises at the Knoxville Zoo in Tennessee.
Nate had some questions.
Michael had some answers.
You have some reading to do.

Q: *How many tortoises live at the zoo?*
A: Eighty-two tortoises! They come from ten different species.

Q: *Tell us about some of your favorite tortoises.*
A: **Al** is an Aldabran tortoise. The Aldabra are four islands in the Indian Ocean. Aldabrans are the largest tortoises in the world! Al is about 125 years old. He weighs 550 pounds.

The flat-tailed tortoises are interesting too. Unlike Al, they are very small. Adult female flat-tails are only about five inches long.

Flat-tails come from Madagascar. That's an island off the coast of Africa. Flat-tails have patterned shells. They blend in well with their natural habitat. They're hard to see! People call them ghosts of the forest.

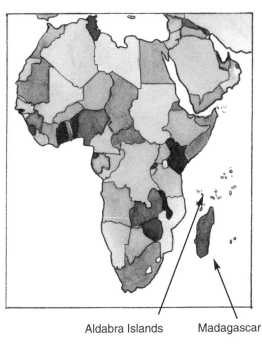

Aldabra Islands   Madagascar

Q: What do tortoises like to eat?

A: Some species graze like cows. They like grass, flowers, leaves, and fruit. Flat-tails come from the forest. They like mushrooms, leaves, and fruit.

Q: How old could Al get? What about the flat-tails?

A: Al could live to be 200 years old! Flat-tails live around 75 years.

Q: Do tortoises play?
A: No.

Q: Where do the tortoises sleep?
A: Some small species sleep in burrows they
   dig. A burrow is something like a rabbit
   hole. Other species sleep in sheltered
   places they find. This helps them hide
   from animals that want to eat them.
   Aldabrans don't have predators. They
   sleep in the open.

Q: *Can tortoises pull their heads, feet, and tails into their shells?*

A: Just their heads. Their legs have scales to protect them.

Q: *How did you get to be a zookeeper?*

A: I've always liked tortoises and other reptiles. I started working for the zoo for free. Then they gave me a part-time job. I've been working here full-time since 2001.

Q: *Is it fun?*

A: I have the best job in the world! There's nothing else I'd rather do.

Have you helped solve all
Nate the Great's mysteries?

❏ **Nate the Great**: Meet Nate, the great detective, and join him as he uses incredible sleuthing skills to solve his first big case.

❏ **Nate the Great Goes Undercover**: Who—or what—is raiding Oliver's trash every night? Nate bravely hides out in his friend's garbage can to catch the smelly crook.

❏ **Nate the Great and the Lost List**: Nate loves pancakes, but who ever heard of cats eating them? Is a strange recipe at the heart of this mystery?

❏ **Nate the Great and the Phony Clue**: Against ferocious cats, hostile adversaries, and a sly phony clue, Nate struggles to prove that he's still the world's greatest detective.

❏ **Nate the Great and the Sticky Case**: Nate is stuck with his stickiest case yet as he hunts for his friend Claude's valuable stegosaurus stamp.

❏ **Nate the Great and the Missing Key**: Nate isn't afraid to look anywhere—even under the nose of his friend's ferocious dog, Fang—to solve the case of the missing key.

❑ **Nate the Great and the Snowy Trail**: Nate has his work cut out for him when his friend Rosamond loses the birthday present she was going to give him. How can he find the present when Rosamond won't even tell him what it is?

❑ **Nate the Great and the Fishy Prize**: The trophy for the Smartest Pet Contest has disappeared! Will Sludge, Nate's clue-sniffing dog, help solve the case and prove he's worthy of the prize?

❑ **Nate the Great Stalks Stupidweed**: When his friend Oliver loses his special plant, Nate searches high and low. Who knew a little weed could be so tricky?

❑ **Nate the Great and the Boring Beach Bag**: It's no relaxing day at the beach for Nate and his trusty dog, Sludge, as they search through sand and surf for signs of a missing beach bag.

❑ **Nate the Great Goes Down in the Dumps**: Nate discovers that the only way to clean up this case is to visit the town dump. Detective work can sure get dirty!

❑ **Nate the Great and the Halloween Hunt**: It's Halloween, but Nate isn't trick-or-treating for candy. Can any of the witches, pirates, and robots he meets help him find a missing cat?

❑ **Nate the Great and the Musical Note**: Nate is used to looking for clues, not listening for them! When he gets caught in the middle of a musical riddle, can he hear his way out?

❏ **Nate the Great and the Stolen Base**: It's not easy to track down a stolen base, and Nate's hunt leads him to some strange places before he finds himself at bat once more.

❏ **Nate the Great and the Pillowcase**: When a pillowcase goes missing, Nate must venture into the dead of night to search for clues. Everyone sleeps easier knowing Nate the Great is on the case!

❏ **Nate the Great and the Mushy Valentine**: Nate hates mushy stuff. But when someone leaves a big heart taped to Sludge's doghouse, Nate must help his favorite pooch discover his secret admirer.

❏ **Nate the Great and the Tardy Tortoise**: Where did the mysterious green tortoise in Nate's yard come from? Nate needs all his patience to follow this slow . . . slow . . . clue.

❏ **Nate the Great and the Crunchy Christmas**: It's Christmas, and Fang, Annie's scary dog, is not feeling jolly. Can Nate find Fang's crunchy Christmas mail before Fang crunches on *him*?

❏ **Nate the Great Saves the King of Sweden**: Can Nate solve his *first-ever* international case without leaving his own neighborhood?

❏ **Nate the Great and Me: The Case of the Fleeing Fang**: A surprise Happy Detective Day party is great fun for Nate until his friend's dog disappears! Help Nate track down the missing pooch, and learn all the tricks of the trade in a special fun section for aspiring detectives.

❑ **Nate the Great and the Monster Mess**: Nate loves his mother's deliciously spooky Monster Cookies, but the recipe has vanished! This is one case Nate and his growling stomach can't afford to lose.

❑ **Nate the Great, San Francisco Detective**: Nate visits his cousin Olivia Sharp in the big city, but it's no vacation. Can he find a lost joke book in time to save the world?

❑ **Nate the Great and the Big Sniff**: Nate depends on his dog, Sludge, to help him solve all his cases. But Nate is on his own this time, because Sludge has disappeared! Can Nate solve the case and recover his canine buddy?

❑ **Nate the Great on the Owl Express**: Nate boards a train to guard Hoot, his cousin Olivia Sharp's pet owl. Then Hoot vanishes! Can Nate find out *whooo* took the feathered creature?